FINDERS KEEPERS

by COURTNEY CARBONE

illustrated by SIMONE BUONFANTINO ★ colors by TOMATO FARM

A Random House PICTUREBACK® Book
Random House 🏠 New York

All rights reserved. Published in the United States by Random House Children's Books, a division of Penguin Random House LLC, 1745 Broadway, New York, NY 10019, and in Canada by Penguin Random House Canada Limited, Toronto. Pictureback, Random House, and the Random House colophon are registered trademarks of Penguin Random House LLC.
randomhousekids.com
dcsuperherogirls.com
dckids.com
ISBN 978-1-5247-6609-2 (trade pbk.) — ISBN 978-1-5247-6610-8 (ebook)
Printed in the United States of America
10 9 8 7 6 5 4 3 2 1

One morning at Super Hero High, Supergirl and Batgirl were up early, putting in some extra time making costumes for the school play. Batgirl used the measuring tape from her Utility Belt to measure the fabric, while Supergirl cut out patterns with her heat vision.

Bolts of fabric toppled from the shelves, startling the heroes. Then they realized something was wrong.

"My cape is gone!" Supergirl yelled.

"And my Utility Belt!" Batgirl exclaimed.

In the gym, some of the students were taking phys ed. Coach Wildcat was teaching them the basics of defense. After the workout, Wonder Woman, Bumblebee, and Hawkgirl went to retrieve their gear from the bleachers.

"Oh, no!" Wonder Woman exclaimed. "My shield is missing!"

"Same with my wrist blasters!" Bumblebee cried.

At the same time, the heroes in Mr. Fox's Weaponomics class were learning how to disarm a sparkly glitter bomb. Harley Quinn and Katana volunteered to go first.

"We have to be very careful," Katana whispered, steadying her sword.

"Careful is my middle name!" Harley replied, raising her mallet over her head.

BAM! There was a giant explosion of color as the bomb went off by itself. Sparkly, shimmery pieces fell down around them.

"My mallet!" Harley cried. "Someone stole it right out of my hands!"

"My sword is gone, too!" Katana yelled.

Meanwhile, in art class, Star Sapphire and Green Lantern took off their power rings and put them aside while they worked.

Without warning, the pottery wheel began to spin out of control! Chunks of sticky clay flew everywhere!

"What happened?" Green Lantern asked.

"I don't know," Star Sapphire replied. "But our power rings are gone!"

In the hallway, the other heroes saw footprints on the floor.
"The chase is on!" Wonder Woman yelled.
"Follow those prints!"

The students followed the footprints outside.
Just ahead, they saw a round orange alien whose multiple arms
were full of the heroes' missing possessions. The heroes were
gaining on him, until a giant spaceship appeared in the sky!

"A spaceship!" Bumblebee exclaimed. "And the alien is getting away!" Batgirl added.

"Not if I can help it," Wonder Woman said, spinning her Lasso over her head. In one quick motion, she captured the alien.

"Why did you steal from us?" Wonder Woman demanded. The little orange alien couldn't resist the Lasso's power. He had to tell the truth.

"I am on an intergalactic scavenger hunt for my master, Larfleeze," he said. "He wishes to have *all* these wonderful trinkets on his home world."

"I think we can find plenty of stuff to make Larfleeze happy," Star Sapphire said.

"Stuff! Wonderful," cheered the alien. "My master loves *stuff*!"

In the school's Lost and Found closet, the alien was able to
collect all the items on his scavenger hunt list. He was overjoyed.
"How can I ever thank you?" he asked.
"Easy!" Supergirl replied. "Next time, just send us your list!"